Will   Irma   Taranee   Cornelia   Hay Lin

GRAPHIC NOVEL #6
FORCES OF CHANGE

W.i.t.ch. 6

Will   Irma   Taranee   Cornelia   Hay Lin

GRAPHIC NOVEL #6
FORCES OF CHANGE

HYPERION PAPERBACKS
FOR CHILDREN
New York

Printed in the United States of America

First Edition
1 3 5 7 9 10 8 6 4 2

ISBN 0-7868-4877-4

Visit www.clubwitch.com

CANDRACAR

LONG AGO, THIS PLACE WAS CREATED TO HOUSE THOSE WHOSE TASK IS TO WATCH OVER OTHER WORLDS AND DIMENSIONS. . . .

. . . A TASK THAT THE ORACLE HAS NEVER FAILED.

ALTHOUGH HIS EYES HAVE OBSERVED BILLIONS OF LIVES, NOTHING SEEMS TO HAVE UPSET HIM. . . .

YET TODAY, SOMETHING IS DIFFERENT. ON HIS FOREHEAD, THERE IS A THIN LINE OF CONCERN.

TODAY, FOR THE FIRST TIME, THE ORACLE IS WORRIED.

MERIDIAN

HAVE YOU MADE UP YOUR MIND YET, YOUR HIGHNESS?

I . . . I'M NOT SURE. ALL YOUR GOWNS ARE SO BEAUTIFUL. . . .

A SPECIAL DAY CALLS FOR A SPECIAL GOWN. . . .

. . . AND YOUR CORONATION WILL DEFINITELY BE A SPECIAL AND UNFORGETTABLE DAY FOR THE ENTIRE CITY.

HMMM . . . WELL, I'LL THINK ABOUT THESE DRESSES FOR A LITTLE WHILE, MASTER JINK. THEN I'LL LET YOU KNOW WHICH ONE.

IF YOU WANT MY OPINION . . .

. . . I WOULD HAVE ASKED FOR IT. WHERE'S MY BROTHER?

3

PRINCE PHOBOS IS MEETING WITH HIS MURMURERS.

I SEE.

AH, LISTEN, CEDRIC . . .

. . . I'VE NOTICED THAT IN PUBLIC, YOU DON'T CALL ME BY NAME. YOU USE THE TITLE "YOUR HIGHNESS". . . .

A COURTESY WORTHY OF A PERSON OF YOUR RANK.

WELL, FROM NOW ON, I'D LIKE YOU TO SHOW ME THE SAME COURTESY IN **PRIVATE** AS WELL.

B—BUT . . . OF COURSE. AS YOU WISH, YOUR HIGHNESS.

THE NERVE OF THAT GIRL. A FEW WEEKS AGO SHE WOULDN'T HAVE DARED TO TREAT ME THIS WAY.

RECENT EVENTS MUST HAVE TRIGGERED SOMETHING IN THAT LITTLE HEAD OF HERS.

I'D BETTER INFORM THE PRINCE IMMEDIATELY. HE'LL WANT TO KNOW OF THIS DEVELOPMENT.

ENLIGHTENED COURT OF MURMURERS, VOICE AND EYES OF THE PRINCE OF PRINCES.

I ASK YOUR LEAVE TO CONSULT WITH OUR POWERFUL LORD.

I WAS EXPECTING YOU, CEDRIC. YOU ALWAYS ARRIVE AT JUST THE RIGHT MOMENT. . . .

. . . JOIN ME WITHOUT FEAR. . . . IN THE ABYSS OF SHADOWS!

. . . ABYSS OF SHAD—

. . . OF SHADOWS . . .

BACK IN HEATHERFIELD...

NO COOKIES THIS TIME?

I'M SORRY, BUT NO. THIS IS AN EMERGENCY MEETING. I JUST RECEIVED SOME UPSETTING NEWS FROM MERIDIAN. A FEW DAYS AGO, ELYON'S CORONATION WAS ANNOUNCED!

IS EATING ALL YOU EVER THINK ABOUT?

HOW DID YOU FIND OUT? DID YOU GO TO METAMOOR?

REALLY?

NO, CORNELIA! I CAME INTO MENTAL CONTACT WITH SOME ACQUAINTANCES WHO ARE STILL THERE.

WOW! OUR FRIEND IS ABOUT TO MAKE IT BIG! I'VE NEVER KNOWN A PRINCESS BEFORE!

...AND WHAT I HEARD ABOUT THE CEREMONY WAS NOT GOOD... NOT GOOD AT ALL!

THE CITY IS FILLED WITH EXCITEMENT AND ANTICIPATION. BOTH THE REBEL GROUPS AND THE CITIZENS OF MERIDIAN EXPECT A GREAT DEAL FROM ELYON . . .

BUT YOU'RE WORRIED THAT PHOBOS IS PLOTTING SOMETHING, RIGHT?

YES, WILL! THE PRINCE IS A CRUEL, POWER-HUNGRY CREATURE. HE WOULD NEVER RELINQUISH THE THRONE TO HIS SISTER— NOT WITHOUT A FIGHT.

I CAN UNDERSTAND THAT. I EVEN FIGHT WITH MY BROTHER ABOUT WHO GETS TO SIT IN THE FRONT SEAT OF THE CAR . . .

SO WHY IS HE GOING THROUGH WITH THE CEREMONY, THEN?

I'VE BEEN ASKING MYSELF THE SAME QUESTION. ELYON NEEDS TO FIGURE IT OUT . . . BUT I DON'T KNOW IF SHE WILL.

THAT POOR GIRL IS ALL ALONE, AND IS UNDER THE INFLUENCE OF PHOBOS AND CEDRIC . . .

NOT AS MUCH AS YOU MAY THINK. ELYON HAS BEEN CHANGING RECENTLY. I KNOW IT.

MAYBE THAT'S EXACTLY WHAT'S MAKING THE PRINCE NERVOUS ENOUGH TO PUSH UP THE CEREMONY. ANNOUNCING THE CORONATION WAS A VERY SUDDEN DECISION.

BUT THEN . . . WHAT CAN WE DO?

I'D LIKE YOU TO KEEP AN EYE ON ELYON AND MAKE SURE THAT SHE DOESN'T GET HURT!

LATER . . .

SHE MAKES IT SOUND LIKE IT'S SO EASY! WE'RE ALREADY UP TO OUR NECKS IN DEALING WITH WHAT'S LEFT OF THE TWELVE PORTALS.

DON'T YOU GET IT? THE PORTALS ARE A SECONDARY CONCERN RIGHT NOW.

IF PHOBOS DESTROYS MERIDIAN, THE ENTIRE VEIL WILL BE BROUGHT DOWN, TOO. THERE'D BE WARS AND UPRISINGS EVERYWHERE.

SO I GUESS WE'LL BE TAKING ANOTHER TRIP TO MONSTROPOLIS, HUH?

SURE LOOKS LIKE IT. IF ONLY WE KNEW HOW TO GET THERE!

OH, NO, THAT'S RIGHT! WITHOUT MY GRANDMOTHER'S MAP, WE'RE PRETTY MUCH STUCK.

WE COULD ALWAYS USE THE PORTAL IN ELYON'S HOUSE.

IT'S TOO DIFFICULT TO GET IN WITHOUT BEING SPOTTED. THOSE TWO SPECIAL AGENTS ARE STILL THERE, REMEMBER?

RIGHT! THOSE SNOOPS HAVE PRACTICALLY PITCHED CAMP AT ELLIE'S PLACE.

DO YOU THINK THEY'LL FIND THE PORTAL?

NO CHANCE! WITH THE WALL I CREATED, THEY'LL NEVER FIND IT! GUARANTEED!

STEP ASIDE, MEDINA . . .

TLALK

DARN IT!

LET'S GIVE IT A REST FOR NOW, MCTIENNAN. YOU CAN HAVE ANOTHER LITTLE CHAT WITH THE WALL TOMORROW MORNING.

I COULD TRY USING DYNAMITE . . .

IF THE BROWN FAMILY EVER COMES BACK, IT WOULD BE NICE TO LET THEM FIND THEIR HOUSE HERE, DON'T YOU THINK?

IF THEY EVER CAME BACK, I'D ASK THEM TO EXPLAIN WHAT'S THE DEAL WITH THIS WALL!

STILL NOTHING, DETECTIVES?

UNFORTUNATELY, NOTHING, LAIR. ALL THE ECHO DETECTOR DID WAS CONFIRM WHAT WE ALREADY KNEW...

...BEHIND THIS WALL IS AN ENORMOUS ROOM THAT FOR SOME REASON DOES NOT APPEAR ON THE BLUEPRINT OF THIS HOUSE.

SURE LOOKS LIKE OUR MISSING FAMILY HAD SOMETHING TO HIDE.

NO DOUBT ABOUT IT...

...AND THEY'VE DONE A REALLY GOOD JOB OF HIDING IT!

THE NEXT DAY, AT SHEFFIELD INSTITUTE...

WE DON'T HAVE ANY OTHER CHOICE, GUYS. WE NEED TO FIND ANOTHER PORTAL.

MY DAD SAYS THOSE TWO COPS ARE GOING TO BE AROUND FOR A LONG TIME.

BUT IT COULD TAKE US WEEKS TO FIND ANOTHER PORTAL. MONTHS! WE DON'T HAVE THAT MUCH TIME.

IF YOU'RE TALKING ABOUT THE TIME YOU HAVE LEFT FOR YOUR LITTLE CHAT, IT HAS DEFINITELY RUN OUT, MISS HALE.

GOTCHA! SEE YOU GUYS AT LUNCH?

ALL RIGHT, OFF TO CLASS. MOVE ALONG, NOW, QUICKLY AND QUIETLY. MAKE YOUR PRINCIPAL A HAPPY WOMAN.

SURE THING. SEE YOU LATER!

WHAT ARE YOU DOING OUT HERE? IN CASE YOU HADN'T NOTICED, CLASS IS THIS WAY!

IT'S OUR RECESS TIME, MRS. KNICKERBOCKER.

IT'S CALLED PHYSICAL EDUCATION, YOU TROGLODYTE!

IT'S SO NICE TO HEAR YOU USE BIG WORDS, URIAH. THE TIME YOU'VE BEEN SPENDING AT THE MUSEUM IS STARTING TO PAY OFF!

HA-HA-HA!

WHAT ARE YOU LAUGHING AT?

SORRY, URIAH!

OLD MUMMY! SHE'S THE ONE WHO SHOULD BE AT THE MUSEUM . . . AS AN EXHIBIT!

COME ON, THE MUSEUM'S NOT THAT BAD.

SHUT UP, KURT! WE WERE SUPPOSED TO WORK THERE FOR THREE MONTHS . . . BUT BECAUSE OF YOU WE'LL BE SPENDING A WHOLE YEAR IN THAT PLACE!

BECAUSE OF ME? WHY IS IT ALWAYS MY FAULT?

WHO'S THE ONE THAT STARTED PLAYING BASEBALL IN THE DINOSAUR HALL?

I—I WAS JUST THE BATTER! LAURENT WAS THE PITCHER!

OKAY! STRIKE TWO, BALL THREE!

NIGEL'S THE ONLY ONE WHO DIDN'T GET IN TROUBLE.

YEAH, MR. GOODY TWO-SHOES DID HIS THREE MONTHS AND GOT OFF CLEAN BECAUSE HE WAS SUCH A GOOD BOY. NOW HE HANGS OUT WITH "DECENT FOLK" . . . LIKE JUDGE COOK'S DAUGHTER.

YEAH! I CAN'T BELIEVE HE CHOSE A GIRL OVER HIS FRIENDS!

YOU KNOW WHAT? I THINK WE OWE OUR OLD FRIEND A LITTLE FAREWELL GIFT.

WHAT DO YOU SAY ABOUT A NICE WATCH?

?

COME ON, BERLIN! YOU CAN DO IT! YOU'RE ALMOST THERE! COME ON!

IS THAT TUB OF LARD BERLIN COMING?

NOT YET.

THIS SHOULD DO THE TRICK.

GO JOIN THE OTHERS AND PRETEND LIKE NOTHING HAPPENED. I'LL CATCH UP WITH YOU IN A MINUTE.

AH, HERE'S NIGEL'S LOCKER . . .

I'VE BEEN THINKING IT OVER, GUYS, AND I MIGHT HAVE THE SOLUTION TO OUR PROBLEM.

I THINK SO. THE PORTAL THAT VATHEK USED TO GET TO HEATHERFIELD A FEW DAYS AGO.*

WHEN WE WENT BACK TO METAMOOR WITH HIM, WE CROSSED THROUGH THE PORTAL IN ELYON'S HOUSE .

*See W.i.t.c.h. #10.

YOU'VE FOUND A WAY TO GET TO MERIDIAN?

. . . WHICH MEANS THAT THERE'S STILL AN OPEN PORTAL SOMEWHERE!

RIGHT! BUT WHERE?

THAT'S THE THING. I DON'T KNOW . . . BUT I FIGURED MAYBE WE COULD USE OUR POWERS TO FIGURE IT OUT.

WANT TO MEET UP AT MY PLACE AFTER SCHOOL?

COUNT ME IN!

SURE, SOUNDS LIKE A PLAN.

RIIING

HUH? THE BELL'S EARLY. WE STILL HAVE TEN MINUTES LEFT FOR LUNCH!

CHECK IT OUT! KNICKERBOCKER'S MAKING AN ANNOUNCEMENT.

WITH ALL DUE RESPECT, MA'AM, I'M TIRED OF BEING TREATED LIKE THIS. WHY DON'T YOU JUST HAVE ME SEARCHED LIKE A CRIMINAL?

LOOK THROUGH MY BACKPACK! OPEN MY LOCKER!

CALM DOWN, URIAH. I DIDN'T MEAN IT LIKE THAT...

OPEN YOURS UP, TOO, KURT! 'CAUSE WE'RE THE BAD GUYS, AREN'T WE?

17

EVERYTHING THAT HAPPENS AROUND HERE IS ALWAYS OUR FAULT! SO GO AHEAD, TAKE A LOOK!

POOR URIAH... I FEEL KIND OF SORRY FOR HIM.

I DIDN'T MEAN TO OFFEND YOU, URIAH, AND I APOLOGIZE IF YOU THOUGHT THAT...

I CAN'T BELIEVE SHE'S FALLING FOR IT!

NO, MA'AM! IF YOU SEARCH ME, THEN YOU HAVE TO SEARCH EVERYONE!

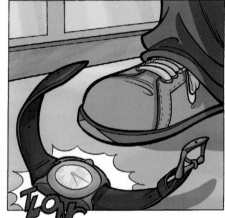

THAT'S MY WATCH!

NIGEL!

B—BUT... BUT...

NIGEL!

OH, NIGEL, HOW COULD YOU?

WAIT... I DIDN'T DO IT!

MY OFFICE, NIGEL. NOW!

WHAT DO I DO NOW?

19

YES?
JUST A MOMENT,
PLEASE . . .

TARANEE?
NIGEL'S ON THE
PHONE.

OH,
REALLY?

WELL,
I DON'T WANT
TO TALK TO
HIM. TELL
HIM I'M NOT
HERE.

HAS SOMETHING
HAPPENED?

NO, NOTHING'S HAPPENED.
JUST TELL HIM I'M NOT
HERE.

IF
YOU SAY
SO . . .

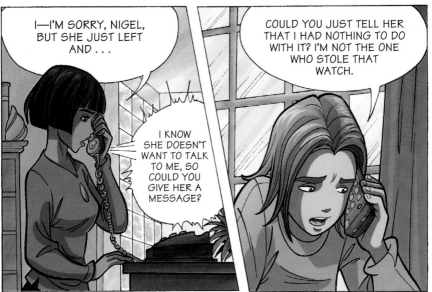

I—I'M SORRY, NIGEL, BUT SHE JUST LEFT AND . . .

I KNOW SHE DOESN'T WANT TO TALK TO ME, SO COULD YOU GIVE HER A MESSAGE?

COULD YOU JUST TELL HER THAT I HAD NOTHING TO DO WITH IT? I'M NOT THE ONE WHO STOLE THAT WATCH.

WATCH? WHAT ARE YOU TALKING ABOUT? NIGEL? HELLO? NIGEL?

CHEER UP, TARANEE . . . IT'S NOT SO BAD . . .

I JUST CAN'T BELIEVE IT. I DON'T WANT TO BELIEVE IT.

BUT WE ALL SAW IT WITH OUR OWN EYES.

VERY HELPFUL, CORNELIA . . .

COULD WE . . . COULD WE CHANGE THE SUBJECT, PLEASE?

SURE, TARANEE . . .

*See W.i.t.c.h. #10.

THE SOUND OF THE TOKEN RINGS THROUGH HAY LIN'S MIND WITH AN ENDLESS ECHO...

IMAGES BEGIN TO APPEAR IN HER MIND, BLURRY AND JUMBLED AT FIRST...

...THEN CLEARER AND CLOSER.

23

I'VE GOT IT!

...IT'S AN AMUSEMENT PARK. THE OLD ABANDONED CARNIVAL JUST OUTSIDE OF HEATHERFIELD.

ARE YOU SURE?

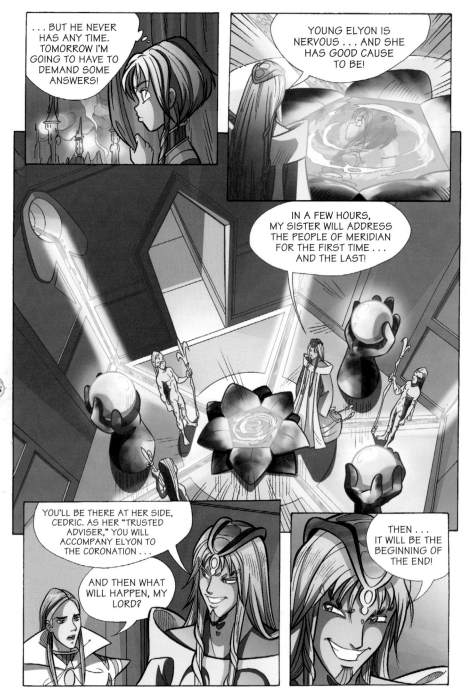

OBSERVE, CEDRIC. A RIVER OF ENERGY ONCE FLOWED THROUGH HERE . . . THE PUREST, MOST POWERFUL RESOURCE IN ALL OF MERIDIAN.

I USED THAT ENERGY TO BECOME STRONGER . . . TO TAKE OVER ENTIRE WORLDS.

THOSE FOOLS FROM CANDRACAR THOUGHT THEY COULD STOP ME BY USING THEIR RIDICULOUS VEIL TO CUT ME OFF FROM THE REST OF THE UNIVERSE.

THEY HAVE CONTAINED ME ONLY TEMPORARILY. THE ENERGY THAT ONCE FLOWED IN ABUNDANCE IS NOW A MERE TRICKLE . . .

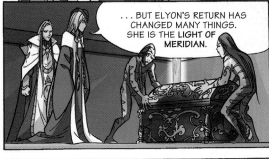

. . . BUT ELYON'S RETURN HAS CHANGED MANY THINGS. SHE IS THE **LIGHT OF MERIDIAN.**

SHE HAS YET TO REALIZE HER LIMITLESS POWERS. I HAVE SPENT A LONG TIME PREPARING FOR THIS DAY. TOMORROW, HER POWER WILL FINALLY BE MINE!

THE LIGHT OF MERIDIAN IS ABOUT TO GO OUT FOREVER!

HOW ARE YOU GOING TO TAKE HER POWERS, MY LORD?

WITH THIS, CEDRIC. THE **CROWN OF LIGHT**!

USING WHAT'S LEFT OF MERIDIAN'S ENERGY RESOURCES, I WILL CREATE A TRAP CAPABLE OF HARNESSING ELYON'S LIFE FORCE.

WHEN I PLACE IT ON HER HEAD, THE CROWN WILL ABSORB ALL HER POWER . . .

KRZZ

KZZZ

ZZZAK

. . . AND, WITH ELYON'S ENERGY AT MY DISPOSAL, I WILL FINALLY DESTROY THE VEIL AND BE FREE ONCE AGAIN!

AND YOU WILL DEAL WITH MY SISTER, GETTING RID OF HER ONCE AND FOR ALL!

BUT . . . YOUR HIGHNESS . . . THE ENTIRE CITY WILL BE THERE TO WITNESS THE CEREMONY. YOUR SISTER IS GREATLY LOVED. WHAT IF THE PEOPLE OF MERIDIAN RISE UP AGAINST US?

THAT WILL BE NO CONCERN OF OURS.

"OKAY! WE'LL MEET YOU OVER AT THE GOLDEN IN HALF AN HOUR!"

I'M SORRY TO BOTHER YOU GUYS . . . BUT THIS IS REALLY SERIOUS.

YOUR FOLKS SAID THAT YOU WERE OUT WITH WILL. SO I CALLED WILL'S PLACE, AND HER MOM GAVE ME HER—

WHATEVER, MARTIN! BEGIN AT THE BEGINNING, AND TELL US EVERYTHING YOU KNOW.

I REALLY WANTED TO TELL YOU EVERYTHING TODAY AT SCHOOL, BUT . . . WELL, I WAS SCARED!

NIGEL HAD NOTHING TO DO WITH THE THEFT THIS MORNING. IT WAS URIAH WHO STOLE BERLIN'S WATCH. I SAW HIM.

BUT . . . WHY DIDN'T YOU TELL THE PRINCIPAL THE TRUTH?

AND GET BEAT UP BY URIAH AND HIS THUGS? THOSE GUYS DON'T KID AROUND . . . BUT I'VE THOUGHT ABOUT IT, AND I CAN'T LET AN INNOCENT PERSON TAKE THE BLAME, EITHER. WHAT SHOULD I DO, IRMA?

WHAT DO YOU THINK? TOMORROW MORNING YOU'RE GOING STRAIGHT TO MRS. KNICKERBOCKER AND TELLING HER EVERYTHING.

"DO YOU TRUST US OR NOT?"

... AND THAT'S WHAT HAPPENED, MA'AM.

I CAN IMAGINE HOW DIFFICULT IT MUST HAVE BEEN FOR YOU TO TELL ME ALL OF THIS, MARTIN. IT'S VERY DECENT OF YOU.

HMMM ... I SEE.

I WANTED YOU TO HEAR THIS IN PERSON, NIGEL. I THINK YOU'VE FOUND A NEW FRIEND.

THANKS, MARTIN.

AS FOR YOU, URIAH ... IS THERE ANYTHING YOU'D LIKE TO SAY FOR YOURSELF?

IT—IT WAS ONLY A JOKE, MA'AM! I WAS JUST KIDDING AROUND!

33

WELL, I HOPE THAT YOU'VE HAD A GOOD LAUGH, BECAUSE YOUR LITTLE PRANK IS GOING TO COST YOU A FIVE-DAY SUSPENSION.

!

PFF! WELL?

THEY'RE LEAVING THE OFFICE.

GUYS, OUR POWERS AREN'T AT THEIR STRONGEST LEVELS WHEN WE HAVEN'T TRANSFORMED...

...BUT THEY'RE MORE THAN ENOUGH TO TAKE CARE OF URIAH AND HIS PALS!

WHATEVER WE DO, WE JUST HAVE TO MAKE SURE WE'RE NOT SEEN.

DON'T WORRY, CORNELIA...

WE'LL USE A LITTLE TRICK I DISCOVERED NOT TOO LONG AGO. A LITTLE SOMETHING CALLED...

...INVISIBILITY!

WOW!

"LET ME SHOW YOU HOW IT WORKS..."

BYE!

SEE YOU TOMORROW, THEN!

OKAY, I'LL CALL YOU LATER.

SO LONG, MARTIN!

SEE YOU AROUND, ROCK!

PSST...
MARTIN!

IF IT'S ME YOU'RE LOOKING FOR, HERE I AM!

U—URIAH!

I SAID I'D MEET YOU AFTER SCHOOL, AND YOU KNOW ME... I'M A GUY WHO KEEPS HIS PROMISES. I NEVER STAND PEOPLE UP, RIGHT, KURT?

UH-HUH...

...IT'S RIGHT HERE IN YOUR APPOINTMENT BOOK, URIAH: "FROM 3:00 TO 3:30— BEAT MARTIN UP."

GOSH, IT'S ALREADY **TWENTY PAST**! IF YOU WANT, WE COULD RESCHEDULE FOR ANOTHER DAY...

YOU SHOULD'VE JUST KEPT YOUR MOUTH SHUT. TOMORROW, IF ANYONE ASKS WHAT HAPPENED TO YOU, JUST TELL THEM YOU FELL DOWN THE STAIRS!

WAIT, URIAH! L—LET'S TALK THIS OVER!

WHAT DO YOU SAY TO FRIDAY, SAME TIME? NOW THAT I'M SUSPENDED, I HAVE LOTS OF SPARE TIME ON MY HANDS!

BUT IT'S NOT MY FAULT! I COULDN'T PRETEND LIKE NOTHING HAPPENED AND LET NIGEL GET IN TROUBLE!

OUCH!

TOC

!

WHO . . . WHO DID THAT?

NOBODY! IT JUST FELL FROM THAT TREE!

COME ON! CAN I THROW ANOTHER ONE AT HIM? JUST ONE?

I SAID NO, IRMA . . .

. . . LEAVE SOME ACTION FOR THE REST OF US!

HEY!

AWWW, YOU'RE NO FUN!

THE CREEP IS GETTING AWAY!

GET HIM!

OKAY, LADIES, THAT'S OUR CUE!

LET'S TEACH THESE BULLIES A LESSON THEY WON'T FORGET!

UGH!

SFRSH

?

WHERE'D HE GO?

OH, I CAN DO BETTER THAN THAT . . .

NICE SHOT, HUH?

. . . WITHOUT EVEN USING MY POWERS!

HA! THE OLD TRIPPEROO WORKS EVERY TIME.

39

YOU MAY HAVE FORGOTTEN ABOUT YOUR FRIENDS . . .

STUMP

OOOF!

. . . BUT WE HAVEN'T FORGOTTEN ABOUT YOU!

EXCUSE ME . . .

TIP TAP

NO ONE TREATS MY BACKPACK LIKE THAT!

SOCK

NICE SHOT, MARTIN!

OW!

BUMP

SORRY I DIDN'T GET HERE SOONER. I STARTED FOLLOWING YOU THE MINUTE YOU LEFT SCHOOL, BUT THEN I LOST TRACK OF YOU.

DON'T APOLOGIZE. YOU SAVED MY FRAMES!

SIGH . . . NIGEL IS SUCH A GREAT GUY!

OKAY, NOW THAT THAT'S OVER AND DONE WITH, WE CAN FINALLY GET DOWN TO BUSINESS.

WE HAVE TO LEAVE FOR MERIDIAN RIGHT AWAY. THERE'S NOTHING LEFT FOR US TO DO HERE.

BY NOW OUR ASTRAL DROPS WILL HAVE GOTTEN BACK HOME . . .

". . . I JUST HOPE THEY DON'T CAUSE AS MUCH TROUBLE AS THEY DID LAST TIME!"

BACK AT THE CARNIVAL . . .

WATCH YOUR STEP. THIS PLACE IS FALLING APART.

IT MUST HAVE BEEN BEAUTIFUL ONCE. MY DAD TOLD ME THAT WHEN HE WAS LITTLE, HE USED TO COME HERE EVERY SUNDAY.

HANG ON! I FEEL SOMETHING!

WE'RE THERE, THEN! WILL'S SIXTH SENSE IS KICKING IN!

THE PORTAL MUST BE IN THERE.

YOU DON'T SOUND SO SURE. BEFORE CRAWLING INTO THAT HOLE I'D LIKE TO HAVE A LITTLE MORE ASSURANCE.

MOVE IT OR LOSE IT, IRMA! WILL HAS NEVER BEEN WRONG BEFORE.

WELL, THERE'S A FIRST TIME FOR EVERYTHING. CAN'T I TAKE ONE OF THE BOATS? THAT SWAMP DOESN'T LOOK VERY INVITING TO ME.

YOU'RE THE ONE WHO CONTROLS WATER. IF YOU DON'T WANT TO GET YOUR FEET WET, WHY DON'T YOU USE YOUR POWERS?

THAT'S WHAT WE'RE ALL ABOUT TO DO. GET READY TO TRANSFORM, GUYS. IT'S TIME TO USE . . .

. . . THE HEART OF CANDRACAR!

AWWW! NOW MY BOOTS ARE FILLING UP WITH MUD.

OH, PLEASE! I FEEL LIKE I'M ON A SECRET MISSION WITH MY GRANDMOTHER. WILL YOU GIVE IT A REST?

CUT IT OUT, BOTH OF YOU, AND TAKE A LOOK AT THAT!

IT'S THE PORTAL! THIS MUST BE WHERE VATHEK CAME THROUGH . . .

WE HAVE TO TALK TO ELYON RIGHT AWAY.

THAT WON'T BE EASY. THE PRINCESS IS IN HER CHAMBERS AND THE MURMURERS ARE ROAMING ALL THROUGH THE CASTLE.

BUT I MIGHT BE ABLE TO HELP YOU . . .

YOU LOOK STUNNING! ONE MORE SECOND, AND WE'LL BE DONE.

I REALLY HOPE SO, MASTER JINK.

HUH? I ASKED THAT WE NOT BE DISTURBED! WHO COULD THAT BE?

LET'S FIND OUT . . . COME IN!

TUMP TUMP TUMP TUMP

PLEASE FORGIVE MY INTRUSION, YOUR HIGHNESS. I BRING YOU A GIFT OF OUR MOST BEAUTIFUL FLOWERS TO ADORN YOUR HAIR . . .

THERE MUST BE SOME MISTAKE. I DIDN'T ASK FOR ANY FLOWERS.

. . . WITH THE BEST WISHES OF WILL AND YOUR OTHER FRIENDS, WHO ARE WAITING FOR YOU IN THE GARDEN.

OH!

BUT . . .
YOUR HIGHNESS?

YOU'VE COME BACK FOR ME!

YES, ELYON, BUT WE DON'T HAVE MUCH TIME, SO LISTEN TO WHAT WE HAVE TO TELL YOU . . .

". . . BEFORE YOU MAKE A MISTAKE!"

THE PROCESSION IS READY, SIR.

EXCELLENT! CALL FOR MY SISTER. SHE WILL WALK AT MY SIDE.

I'M ALREADY HERE, PHOBOS.

ARE YOU EXCITED? THE LONG-AWAITED MOMENT HAS FINALLY ARRIVED . . .

. . . AND THE CROWN WILL SOON BE YOURS.

". . . I JUST HOPE I'M WORTHY, MY BROTHER."

LONG LIVE ELYON!

YES . . .

LONG LIVE THE LIGHT OF MERIDIAN!

LONG LIVE THE PRINCESS!

A KINGDOM THAT FOR TOO LONG HAS BEEN DEPRIVED OF ITS RIGHTFUL QUEEN . . .

... AND WRONGFULLY RULED BY A BROTHER TOO LONG DEPRIVED OF HIS BELOVED SISTER!

AT LEAST HE'S BEING HONEST . . .

SHHH!

MAY YOUR ETERNAL POWER ILLUMINATE THE SPIRIT AND THE PATH OF YOUR LOYAL SUBJECTS!

ELYON . . . IT IS WITH GREAT PRIDE AND JOY THAT I OFFER YOU THIS CROWN.

NO LONGER WILL YOU BE CALLED PRINCESS OF MERIDIAN . . .

. . . BECAUSE YOU WILL NO LONGER BE AMONG US! **HA-HA-HA!**

FIZZZ-ZZZZAP!

AAAAYEEEEEEEH!

W—WHAT'S HAPPENING?

IT'S A TRAP!

I'M SORRY, MY DEAR, SWEET ELYON . . . BUT IN THE END, IT'S BETTER THIS WAY. YOU'RE SO YOUNG. YOU WOULD HAVE ENDED UP WASTING YOUR IMMENSE POWER . . .

FZZK!

FZZZZ!

TUMP

. . . WHILE I . . . I KNOW HOW TO USE IT!

SIR! THE CROWD IS FURIOUS!

LET THEM YELL, CEDRIC!

TRAITOR! TRAITOR!

PHOBOS IS A MONSTER!

CRIMINAL!

VILLAIN!

COME ON, GIRLS. WE CAN'T LET PHOBOS GET AWAY!

NO! LEAVE THE PRINCE TO ME.

AH, YES, CALEB. I'VE HEARD YOUR NAME MENTIONED A GREAT DEAL LATELY. SO I GUESS IT'S TRUE. YOU'VE GONE AGAINST YOUR MASTER.

AND TO THINK THAT YOU WERE ONCE A POOR MURMURER. . . .

WRONG! I WAS A MURMURER CAPABLE OF REASON. WHEN I FINALLY OPENED MY EYES I KNEW RIGHT AWAY WHAT SIDE I SHOULD BE ON.

YOU'RE NOT MASTER OF ANYTHING, PHOBOS, AND DEFINITELY NOT MASTER OF ME. NOTHING YOU SEE AROUND YOU IS YOURS.

A MURMURER WITH A WILL OF ITS OWN IS A MISTAKE. . . . AND THERE'S ONLY ONE THING TO DO WITH MISTAKES!

AHHH!

55

PHOBOS IS ATTACKING CALEB. I HAVE TO HELP HIM!

LOOK OUT, CORNELIA!

YOUR SOLDIERS WILL NEVER STOP THE REBELLION. OUR VICTORY IS AT HAND!

THAT MAY BE. . . .

. . . BUT YOU WON'T LIVE LONG ENOUGH TO SEE IT FOR YOURSELF!

AAAAAGH!

YOU'VE GONE BEYOND MY CONTROL. . . . YOU'VE BECOME THE LEADER OF THE DESPERATE GROUP OF REBELLIOUS METAMOORIANS. . . . YOU BROUGHT THEM TOGETHER AND TURNED THEM INTO A THREAT AGAINST ME. . . .

AHHHHH! S—STOP!

AND FOR THIS, I WILL PUNISH YOU, CALEB. I CREATED YOU AS A MURMURER. . . .

NNNH . . .

. . . AND SO A MURMURER YOU SHALL BE AGAIN. . . . IN ITS MOST PRIMITIVE FORM!

57

CALEEEEEEB! NOOOOOO!!!

59

MERIDIAN.
JUST A LITTLE WHILE AGO,
THIS CITY FELT THE WRATH
OF PHOBOS.

THE PRINCE OF METAMOOR
FORCED HIS SUBJECTS TO
LOOK INTO THE DEPTHS OF
HIS BLACK HEART . . .

. . . AND WHAT THEY SAW
WAS HORRIFYING.

PHOBOS'S HEART WAS A
DARK, EMPTY PLACE.

WE'VE GOT TO DO SOMETHING. THESE PEOPLE ARE EXPECTING US TO HELP THEM— ESPECIALLY YOU, ELYON.

AFTER ALL, YOU'RE THEIR PRINCESS NOW.

BUT I AM A PRINCESS WITHOUT A THRONE.

MAYBE, BUT YOU HAVE SOMETHING BETTER— GREAT POWERS.

FATHER! MOTHER!

OH, ELYON. AT LAST, WE CAN BE TOGETHER AGAIN.

I SEE WHERE ELYON GOT HER GREAT LOOKS.

STOP JOKING AROUND, IRMA. YOU KNOW THOSE ARE HER ADOPTIVE PARENTS. THEY WERE THE ONES WHO TOOK HER AWAY FROM HERE—TO KEEP HER SAFE.

AFTER SUCH A LONG TIME, I STILL DON'T KNOW WHAT TO CALL YOU!

YOU KNEW US AS FATHER AND MOTHER. . . .

. . . BUT MY REAL NAME IS ALBORN! I WAS ONCE COMMANDER OF THE ROYAL GUARD OF MERIDIAN!

AND I'M MIRIADEL! I WAS A CAPTAIN IN THE ARMY!

GREAT! YOU CAN HELP US ORGANIZE THE DEFENSE AGAINST PHOBOS'S SOLDIERS.

WELL, I DON'T KNOW...

PLEASE! THESE PEOPLE ARE READY TO DO ANYTHING YOU ASK THEM.

WE HAVE TO UNITE AGAINST PHOBOS! IF WE DON'T STAND UP FOR OURSELVES NOW...

...WE'LL BE CONDEMNED TO SUFFER FOREVER!

THEN LET'S DO IT!

69

THE KEY TO VICTORY LIES IN THE CROWN OF LIGHT.

ELYON MUST WEAR THE CROWN TO ACHIEVE HER FULL POWER.

SHE WILL NEED ALL HER POWERS TO BATTLE PHOBOS.

SO WHAT ARE WE WAITING FOR? LET'S GO TO THE CASTLE AND GET THE CROWN FROM PHOBOS.

YES! TO THE CASTLE!

NOT SO FAST, MY FRIENDS. I'M AFRAID IT WON'T BE SO EASY.

THOOM THOOM THOOM!

THE ANNIHILATORS ARE GETTING CLOSE.

THEN WE'D BETTER GET THIS SHOW ON THE ROAD.

YOU GIRLS NEED TO BE CAREFUL. THIS IS GOING TO BE A DANGEROUS MISSION.

DON'T WORRY ABOUT US, VATHEK. WE'LL BE FINE.

IN FACT, WHEN WE'RE HAVING OUR VICTORY CELEBRATION, I WANT TO SEE YOUR BIG, BLUE FACE IN THE FRONT ROW CHEERING FOR US, GOT IT?

VATHEK, BEFORE WE LEAVE . . .

PAK

. . . I WANT TO ENTRUST YOU WITH THIS. YOU CAN GIVE IT BACK TO ME WHEN THIS WHOLE MESS IS OVER WITH.

IT'S IN EXCELLENT HANDS, CORNELIA.

GOOD LUCK, ELYON!

MERIDIAN IS IN RUINS! I'VE DESTROYED EVERYTHING!

ABSORBING MY SISTER'S POWERS SHOULD HAVE BEEN SO SIMPLE . . . IT WOULD HAVE BEEN MY ULTIMATE VICTORY.

YET I FAILED! I FAILED TO BREAK HER WILL, JUST AS I FAILED TO BREAK THIS CROWN . . .

THE FAULT LIES ONLY IN THE SPELL CAST ON THE CROWN.

NO, CEDRIC, THE FAULT IS ALL MINE! I USED UP ALL THE ENERGY I CONSUMED FROM METAMOOR.

AND NOW IT'S ALL OVER . . .

NO, YOUR HIGHNESS, DON'T SAY THAT.

BUT I WILL NOT GO DOWN WITHOUT A FIGHT! IF I CAN'T HAVE THIS CITY, THEN NO ONE WILL!

I WILL BATTLE ELYON. THE VICTOR'S PRIZE WILL BE THE CROWN OF LIGHT.

A CROWN THAT I NOW PLACE IN YOUR CARE.

I KNOW. YOU'RE AFRAID YOU WON'T BE ABLE TO PROTECT IT, BUT HAVE NO FEAR. I WILL MAKE SURE YOU ARE WELL EQUIPPED FOR THE TASK.

YOUR HIGHNESS, I . . .

I STILL HAVE ENOUGH POWER TO PLAY THIS GAME TO THE VERY END.

AND I WILL FOLLOW YOU ALL THE WAY, MY LORD.

YOU HAVE BEEN VERY FAITHFUL, CEDRIC. IF ALL GOES ACCORDING TO PLAN, YOU WILL BE HANDSOMELY REWARDED.

HELP ME SUCCEED, AND AT LONG LAST YOU WILL BE ADMITTED INTO MY COURT OF MURMURERS.

I AM AT YOUR SERVICE, YOUR HIGHNESS!

GET READY, CEDRIC! YOU ARE ABOUT TO ENTER A NEW EXISTENCE. GET READY, CEDRIC! YOU ARE ABOUT TO ENTER A NEW EXISTENCE.

WZ-ZZZAM

UGHH!

AHHHHH!

KZZZ-ZZZAW

PREPARE TO BE REBORN, STRONGER AND MORE POWERFUL!

MEANWHILE, IN THE STREETS OF MERIDIAN...

THE REBELS ARE CLOSE. I HEAR SOMETHING.

IT'S ABOUT TIME. WE'VE SEARCHED EVERY NEIGHBORHOOD AND FOUND NOTHING.

FOR PHOBOS WILLS IT SO!

RRAAARGH!

KRAZZZAAK

YES, THE GOWN'S TRAIL LEADS RIGHT DOWN HERE.

OPEN THAT DRAIN COVER!

AH, I WASN'T MISTAKEN...

I DIDN'T THINK THEY'D FALL INTO OUR TRAP!

WHOOOOOSH

I WASN'T EVEN SURE THEY'D EVEN FIND THEIR WAY DOWN HERE.

FROST AND HIS GOONS ARE GOING TO BE SWIMMING AROUND THE CANALS OF MERIDIAN FOR SOME TIME!

". . . AND WHO KNOWS? A LITTLE DIP MIGHT JUST BRING THEM TO THEIR SENSES."

YEOOOW!

FSHAKAM

EEEEEEK!

AAAARRGH!

SPLASH

THEY MADE US LOOK LIKE FOOLS!

I KNOW!

THOSE WRETCHED REBELS GOT AWAY...

AND EVEN WORSE, I DIDN'T FIND ELYON!

I—I DON'T KNOW IF I CAN DO IT.

OF COURSE YOU CAN DO IT, ELYON. AND WE'LL BE RIGHT THERE WITH YOU.

NOW THAT WE'RE HERE, I'M A LITTLE SCARED . . . I DON'T KNOW IF I'LL BE ABLE TO STAND UP TO PHOBOS!

OH, COME ON! ALL YOU HAVE TO DO IS GO IN, KICK HIS BUTT, GET THE CROWN BACK, AND COME OUT AGAIN.

DON'T WORRY, ELYON. WE CAN TAKE THE PRINCE BY SURPRISE.

I BET HE STILL HASN'T GOTTEN OVER THE SHOCK HE HAD AT THE CORONATION.

THE ASTRAL DROP WE CREATED WORKED LIKE A CHARM.

IT WAS A GREAT IDEA! HE HAD NO CLUE IT WAS A FAKE. I GOT TO SEE HIS TRUE COLORS, THE FACE BEHIND THE MASK . . .

. . . AND FROM THE LOOK ON HIS FACE, I DON'T THINK HE LIKED OUR LITTLE TRICK VERY MUCH!

I KNOW! YOU RUINED HIS HORRIBLE LITTLE SHOW.

YOU THOUGHT THAT WAS HORRIBLE? YOU SHOULD'VE SEEN HAY LIN'S CHRISTMAS PLAY!

IT WAS SO AWFUL THAT AT THE END, THE AUDIENCE WAS THROWING EGGS BY THE DOZEN!

HA-HA-HA!

ENOUGH!

HUH?

?

THERE YOU ARE! I'VE BEEN EXPECTING YOU.

I WAS ALMOST AFRAID YOU WOULDN'T SHOW UP. THE PRINCE WAS FURIOUS WHEN HE GOT BACK TO THE CASTLE. I HEARD THAT THERE WAS A REVOLT IN THE CITY. IS THAT TRUE?

YES, AND WE'LL TELL YOU ALL ABOUT IT WHEN THE TIME IS RIGHT. BUT RIGHT NOW YOU HAVE TO LEAVE THE CASTLE!

IT WON'T BE SAFE FOR YOU TO STAY HERE WHEN WE BATTLE PHOBOS.

LEAVE? NEVER! I CAN'T ABANDON MY GARDEN. I CAN'T LEAVE THESE ROSES.

WILL TOLD ME ABOUT THESE ROSES. EACH ONE CONTAINS THE SPIRIT OF A PERSON WITHIN IT.

IT'S SO CRUEL...

YES, IT PAINS ME WHEN I THINK ABOUT THE SUFFERING MY BROTHER HAS INFLICTED ON MY PEOPLE. BUT I PROMISE YOU THAT...

LOOK OUT!

FWOOOM

CRASH

WHA—!

"PRIDE."

"COURAGE."

"FREEDOM!"

PHOBOS THOUGHT THAT IT WOULD BE EASY TO TAKE ADVANTAGE OF HIS SISTER AND OF THE PEOPLE OF MERIDIAN.

BUT HE UNDERESTIMATED THEIR STRENGTH AND RESOLVE.

THE CONGREGATION WILL NOT INTERVENE. WE WILL WAIT CALMLY AND SEE HOW THESE EVENTS UNFOLD . . .

THERE'S SOMETHING HE'S NOT TELLING US. WE SHOULD NOT STAND AROUND HERE TALKING WHILE THE GUARDIANS COULD BE IN DANGER.

IF PHOBOS DEFEATS ELYON, NOTHING WILL STOP HIM FROM TAKING OVER THE PRINCESS'S POWERS, AND IF THAT HAPPENS . . .

. . .THEN WE WILL BEGIN TO WORRY. BUT WE CANNOT SAY WHAT WILL HAPPEN . . .

NOW YOU'RE BEGINNING TO SOUND LIKE THE ORACLE, YAN LIN.

I SPEAK ONLY AS A GRANDMOTHER WHO KNOWS HER GRANDDAUGHTER, MY OLD FRIEND.

I WAS ONCE A GUARDIAN MYSELF, AND I ASSURE YOU THAT HAY LIN AND HER FRIENDS ARE STRONGER THAN YOU THINK.

"AND SOON PHOBOS IS GOING TO DISCOVER THAT AS WELL!"

WOW!

NICE DIGS, ELYON!

YES, BUT I REALLY MISS HEATHERFIELD SOMETIMES . . .

THAT'S PERFECT. WE CAN SWAP! AS SOON AS I GET BACK, I'LL TALK TO MY FOLKS, AND . . .

SHHH! LISTEN.

WHAT? I DON'T HEAR ANYTHING . . . EXCEPT FOR A CREEPY SILENCE!

IT'S NOT A SOUND . . . IT'S LIKE A VIBRATION. IT'S COMING FROM THAT HALL AT THE TOP OF THE STAIRS.

THAT'S THE THRONE HALL.

BINGO! LET'S KEEP OUR EYES PEELED AND MOVE QUIETLY.

ELYON

ELYON

!

HERE I AM, PHOBOS.

AH, HERE SHE IS, THE HEIR TO THE THRONE. THIS IS WHAT YOU'RE HERE FOR, ISN'T IT? WHAT ARE YOU WAITING FOR? TAKE IT. IT'S YOURS.

I DON'T WANT TO FIGHT YOU, PHOBOS. I JUST WANT ALL OF THIS MADNESS TO STOP, AND FOR YOU TO GIVE UP AND STAND TRIAL.

HMMM . . . A TEMPTING OFFER . . .

I, ON THE OTHER HAND, HAVE SOMETHING ELSE IN MIND. WHAT DO YOU SAY TO A DUEL?

WE AREN'T HERE TO PLAY GAMES WITH YOU, PHOBOS.

I WASN'T TALKING TO YOU, LITTLE GIRL!

WHAT KIND OF DUEL DID YOU HAVE IN MIND?

DON'T DO IT, ELYON!

A BATTLE OF MAGIC POWERS, NO HOLDS BARRED. IF YOU WIN, MERIDIAN WILL BE YOURS.

BUT IF YOU ARE DEFEATED, YOU MUST PUT ON THE CROWN OF LIGHT SO THAT I CAN ABSORB ALL YOUR POWERS.

WHY SHOULD I TRUST YOU? YOU'VE NEVER BEEN HONEST WITH ME!

I WAS WRONG ABOUT YOU, DEAR SISTER. I SHOULD HAVE GOTTEN RID OF YOU A LONG TIME AGO. IF I HAD, WE WOULDN'T BE HERE TALKING NOW.

THIS IS WHAT IT HAS COME DOWN TO. I HAVE NOTHING LEFT TO LOSE. MY POWERS ARE GROWING WEAKER . . .

. . . WHILE YOUR POWER IS READY TO EXPLODE. THE ODDS ARE IN YOUR FAVOR, ELYON.

I'M OFFERING YOU THE POSSIBILITY TO RISE TO THE THRONE, TO BE HAILED AS THE SAVIOR OF METAMOOR.

THE ONE AND ONLY ELYON. THE LIGHT OF MERIDIAN. IT HAS A NICE RING TO IT . . .

DON'T LISTEN TO HIM, ELYON!

LET'S DO IT, THEN. WHEN I HAVE DEFEATED YOU, YOU'RE GOING TO PAY FOR EVERYTHING YOU'VE DONE!

AH, SUCH A PROUD FIGHTING SPIRIT. THAT'S THE ELYON I KNOW!

WILL! WE CAN'T JUST LET HER FIGHT HIM.

YOU'RE RIGHT. WHEN I GIVE THE SIGNAL, WE'LL ATTACK PHOBOS ALL TOGETHER. READY?

NOW!

KA-ZAM

FOOLISH GIRLS!

OOOH!

BDUMP

UGH!

THIS BATTLE HAS NOTHING TO DO WITH YOU. IT'S A FAMILY MATTER. GET LOST!

AN OLD FRIEND IS EAGERLY AWAITING YOUR ARRIVAL . . . IN THE ABYSS OF SHADOWS.

WHAT'S HAPPENING? WE'RE BEING SUCKED DOWN INTO . . .

WZZZ-ZZZZ

ELYON!

CORNELIA! NO!

AAAGH! WHERE ARE WE GOING?

STRAIGHT DOWN INTO THE DEPTHS OF YOUR NEW NIGHTMARE!

THAT VOICE!

IT SOUNDS LIKE CEDRIC'S.

AND IT IS!

CEDRIC? WHERE ARE YOU? WHAT HAPPENED TO YOUR VOICE? IT SOUNDS LIKE YOU SWALLOWED A PORCUPINE OR SOMETHING...

HELLO AGAIN, GUARDIANS. WHAT'S WRONG? DON'T YOU RECOGNIZE YOUR OLD FRIEND?

!

AAAH!

FOR CENTURIES, THIS CLOCK MARKED THE PASSAGE OF TIME IN MERIDIAN . . .

BUT AS THE CITY BURNS, THE CLOCK'S HANDS MOVE NO MORE.

IF THAT CLOCK COULD STRIKE ONCE AGAIN . . .

. . . IT WOULD SIGNAL THE ARRIVAL OF THE HOUR OF TRUTH FOR FIVE YOUNG GUARDIANS.

WE'LL SEE ABOUT THAT, CEDRIC!

DON'T BOTHER TO RUN AND HIDE, YOU INSOLENT VERMIN. YOU'LL NEVER ESCAPE!

HA! IS THAT ALL YOU CAN DO?

BZAP

SHACK

HAY LIN!

YOUR BLOWS DON'T EVEN SCRATCH ME. I'M STRONGER THAN ALL OF YOU PUT TOGETHER.

OW, MY HEAD. THAT OVERGROWN ROACH REALLY PACKS A PUNCH . . .

HEY, WHAT'S THAT? NO WAY! IT'S THE CROWN OF LIGHT!

GUYS, TAKE A LOOK AT WHAT I FOUND! IT'S ELYON'S CROWN!

DON'T TOUCH THAT!

94

HUH? WHAT'S HAPPENING? THAT ECHOING VOICE SHAKING THE GROUND...

....BUT YOU AND I ALSO HAVE OUR OWN SCORE TO SETTLE. UNTIL THE BITTER END, DEAR SISTER!

UNTIL THE BITTER END...

IT'S ONLY CEDRIC TAKING HIS WELL-DESERVED REVENGE ON YOUR FRIENDS...

I NEVER WANTED IT TO COME TO THIS, ELYON. YOU WERE THE ONE WHO MADE THINGS DIFFICULT.

I ONLY OPENED MY EYES, PHOBOS. I SAW THE SUFFERING GOING ON OUTSIDE THIS CASTLE, AND I REALIZED IT WAS ALL YOUR FAULT.

WHAT YOU CALL MY FAULT I CALL AMBITION. THIS WORLD WAS BRIMMING WITH MAGICAL ENERGY! I MERELY TOOK WHAT WAS RIGHTFULLY MINE.

AND WHEN I ABSORB YOUR IMMENSE POWERS, I AM GOING TO DESTROY THE VEIL AND CROSS THE THRESHOLD OF MERIDIAN, ON TO NEW CONQUESTS.

SORRY TO DISAPPOINT YOU, DEAR BROTHER...

...BUT THERE ARE GOING TO BE A FEW CHANGES TO YOUR PLANS!

IT'S USELESS TO TRY TO RESIST ME, ELYON. YOU CAN'T ESCAPE YOUR DESTINY.

MY DESTINY IS TO RISE TO THE THRONE OF MERIDIAN. IT IS MY BIRTHRIGHT, WHICH YOU TRIED TO STEAL FROM ME.

KRZZZASH

VERY FUNNY! SINCE WHEN DO OLDER BROTHERS HAVE TO TAKE ORDERS FROM LITTLE SISTERS?

SINCE NOW!

BADOOM

MY GOODNESS!

ALBORN! DO YOU HEAR THE BATTLE RAGING IN THE CASTLE?

I DO, MY FRIEND! AT THIS POINT, THERE IS NOTHING MORE WE CAN DO.

OUR BATTLE WAS TO DEFEAT PHOBOS'S ARMY— AND WE WON!

THE FUTURE OF MERIDIAN NOW LIES IN THE HANDS OF THOSE GIRLS!

"AS HAVE YOUR STUPID FRIENDS!"

DONE DEAL, CEDRIC!

I WON'T TELL YOU THIS AGAIN, GUARDIAN! GET AWAY FROM THERE!

BUT DO YOU MIND IF I TAKE A LITTLE SOUVENIR BEFORE I GO?

RAAAAARGH!

I'VE GOT IT, GUYS!

RRRR . . . YOU SHOULDN'T HAVE DONE THAT!

CEDRIC.

YOUR HIGHNESS!

ELYON HAS BEEN DEFEATED. RID YOURSELF OF THOSE LITTLE GIRLS AND BRING MY CROWN TO ME IMMEDIATELY!

I . . . RRRR . . . AT ONCE, SIR!

HEAR THAT? THE PRINCE HAS DESTROYED YOUR FRIEND, AND NOW YOU'RE GOING TO JOIN HER!

IF THAT WORM HURT ELYON, I SWEAR I'LL . . .

CALM DOWN, CORNELIA. HE'S JUST TRYING TO SCARE US.

TARANEE, DO YOU THINK YOU COULD USE YOUR TELEPATHY TO CONTACT ELYON? WE HAVE TO FIND OUT HOW SHE IS.

I'LL CERTAINLY TRY. I NEED TO FOCUS ALL MY ENERGY.

GREAT! IN THE MEANTIME, WE'LL KEEP CEDRIC OCCUPIED.

COME ON, GUYS! LET'S TEACH HIM A LESSON HE'LL NEVER FORGET.

99

ELYON . . . ELYON.

ELYON . . . ELYON.

"ELYON, WHERE ARE YOU?"

IS—IS ANYONE THERE? CAN ANYBODY HEAR ME?

TARANEE.
I'M OVER HERE!

CAN YOU
HEAR ME?
ANSWER ME,
ELYON.

TARANEE . . .

I'M USING TELEPATHY
TO CONTACT YOU, ELYON.
ANSWER BY CONCENTRATING
YOUR THOUGHTS REALLY
HARD. ARE YOU OKAY?

I'M BEING
HELD PRISONER
SOMEWHERE . . .
I FAINTED, BUT I
THINK I'M STILL IN
ONE PIECE.

GREAT!
WITHOUT THE
CROWN, PHOBOS
CANNOT HARM
ME!

RIGHT!

RAAARGH!

BUT IT LOOKS LIKE CEDRIC
HAS NO INTENTION OF
LETTING US TAKE IT
OUT OF HERE.

GOOD.
WE'RE STILL
BATTLING
CEDRIC . . .

. . . AND
HAY LIN
JUST FOUND
THE CROWN
OF LIGHT!

WELL?

EVERYTHING'S OKAY.
ELYON IS BEING HELD
PRISONER. SHE FAINTED,
BUT SHE'S NOT DEFEATED.
PHOBOS WANTS HER
ALIVE, AT LEAST UNTIL
HE'S GOT HIS
HANDS ON THE
CROWN.

CRA-ZAK

THE CROWN! THAT'S THE ONLY THING THAT CAN HELP US PUT AN END TO THIS MESS.

RAAARGH!

KRRR-KRRR-RRRR ADOOM

ELYON NEEDS THE CROWN TO ACHIEVE HER FULL POWER...

RAAARGH!

BADOOM

...BUT IT'S COMPLETELY USELESS AS LONG AS PHOBOS'S DEADLY SPELL REMAINS CAST ON IT.

BUT IF THE SPELL WERE BROKEN...

HUH?

I'M SO DUMB. WHY DIDN'T I THINK OF IT BEFORE?

ENOUGH OF THIS FIGHTING, CEDRIC. YOU WANT THE CROWN? TAKE IT!

UM, WILL...

GRRRRR... SO YOU'RE FINALLY GIVING UP, ARE YOU?

THE GUY'S OUT COLD.

BUT IT'S NOT OVER YET. THERE MIGHT BE REMNANTS OF THE SPELL ON THE CROWN...

...THERE'S ONLY ONE THING TO DO.

FOCUS YOUR POWERS LIKE NEVER BEFORE. THE HEART OF CANDRACAR HAS DEFEATED PHOBOS BEFORE...

...IT'LL DO THE SAME THING TO HIS SPELL. NOW!

ONE AFTER THE OTHER, THE FIVE GIRLS CHANNEL THEIR POWERS INTO THE CROWN.

SLOWLY BUT SURELY, SOMETHING INCREDIBLE STARTS TO HAPPEN.

MMMMM M MM MMMMMMM

I BELIEVE THIS IS YOURS.

GUYS! AM I GLAD TO SEE YOU!

CEDRIC!

P-THUMP!

SIR, I . . .

SILENCE, INCOMPETENT FOOL! YOU WEREN'T CAPABLE OF DESTROYING THE GUARDIANS OF THE VEIL . . .

. . . SO I SHALL HAVE TO DEAL WITH THEM MYSELF. YOUR TIME HAS COME, GUARDIANS. ARE YOU READY?

NO, PHOBOS. WE WON'T FIGHT YOU.

WE'LL LEAVE THAT TO THE NEW QUEEN OF MERIDIAN.

GO ON, ELYON. SHOW HIM WHO'S BOSS.

I DON'T . . .

THERE ARE NO WORDS TO DESCRIBE WHAT HAPPENS NEXT . . .

THE CROWN AND ITS RIGHTFUL BEARER UNITE IN A BURST OF ABSOLUTE POWER . . .

THE DARKNESS DISSOLVES, AND A NEW DAY BEGINS . . .

THE DAY PHOBOS HAS ALWAYS FEARED . . .

THE DAY THE PEOPLE OF METAMOOR HAVE ALWAYS HOPED FOR . . .

THE LIGHT OF MERIDIAN HAS RETURNED TO SHINE ONCE AGAIN.

AND NEVER AGAIN SHALL ANYONE EXTINGUISH HER SPLENDOR.

GO AHEAD, LITTLE SISTER. I AM NOT AFRAID. DO WHAT YOU MUST.

FOR ALL OF THE PAIN YOU'VE INFLICTED ON THE PEOPLE OF MERIDIAN, I WANT ONLY ONE THING . . .

TO FORGET ALL ABOUT YOU.

CAN WE HUG YOU, OR WOULD A BOW BE MORE APPROPRIATE?

DON'T BE SILLY. I'M ROYALTY NOW. I'M GLOWING WITH THE LIGHT OF MERIDIAN . . .

. . . I HAVE TO MAINTAIN THE PROPER DECORUM!

UMM . . . MAYBE YOU SHOULD TAKE A LOOK DOWN THERE, YOUR HIGHNESS.

THERE SHE IS!

IT'S ELYON!

THE PRINCESS HAS WON! PHOBOS IS DEFEATED!

LONG LIVE THE NEW RULER OF MERIDIAN!

LOOK AT ALL THOSE PEOPLE! WHAT—WHAT DO I DO NOW?

I'M NO EXPERT AT CORONATIONS, BUT I THINK YOU SHOULD SAY SOMETHING TO THEM.

YOU'RE THEIR QUEEN NOW, ELYON.

QUEEN?

GO ON!

FRIENDS . . . PEOPLE OF MERIDIAN . . .

MY BROTHER'S REIGN IS FINISHED FOREVER, AND I . . . I ASK YOUR FORGIVENESS FOR EVERYTHING YOU'VE SUFFERED.

THE FIRST THING I WANT TO DO IS SHARE SOMETHING WITH ALL OF YOU. SOMETHING THAT MY BROTHER STOLE. THERE WAS A TIME WHEN A MAGICAL FORCE FLOWED THROUGH THIS LAND . . .

. . . AND SO I CALL UPON MY POWERS TO MAKE IT FLOW ONCE AGAIN!

K-WAAAAM

THE GROUND IS HEATING UP!

MAY EVIL DISAPPEAR FROM THIS WORLD FOREVER. MAY EVERY SPELL CAST BY PHOBOS BE REMOVED. MAY MERIDIAN RETURN TO ITS FORMER SPLENDOR.

FWOOOOSH

ELYON'S POWER SPREADS THROUGH THE ENTIRE CITY, THROUGH EVERY STREET, EVERY CORNER. EVERY ROSE. THE WALLS OF THE FLOWERY PRISONS BURST OPEN . . .

KZZZZZZZ

. . . THE TIME HAS FINALLY COME FOR THEIR PRISONERS TO EMERGE INTO FREEDOM.

KZZZZZ

THE TIME HAS COME FOR MERIDIAN TO COME BACK TO LIFE.

DALTAR!

DADDY!

HAPPINESS.

GRRR! ALL THAT POWER WASTED ON THOSE WORTHLESS WRETCHES. YOU'RE JUST A FOOLISH LITTLE GIRL.

PERHAPS, PHOBOS . . .

. . . BUT I'M A FOOLISH LITTLE GIRL WHO'S FINALLY HAPPY.

BE CAREFUL, PHOBOS. AS MY GRANDMA USED TO SAY, "IF YOU DON'T UNDERSTAND YOUR PUNISHMENT, YOU DESERVE ANOTHER ONE"!

THIS IS FOR YOU, CORNELIA. IT'S FROM VATHEK.

OH, THANK YOU!

I DON'T KNOW WHAT TO SAY TO YOU ALL. WITHOUT YOU, NONE OF THIS WOULD HAVE BEEN POSSIBLE.

WE DID ONLY WHAT HAD TO BE DONE.

WILL YOU BE COMING BACK TO HEATHERFIELD?

I DON'T THINK SO, CORNELIA. THIS IS MY WORLD NOW. BUT YOU'LL COME TO VISIT ME, WON'T YOU?

YOU CAN COUNT ON IT! BUT . . . HEY! WHAT'S HAPPENING?

DON'T LOOK AT ME! I DIDN'T TOUCH ANYTHING.

EVERYTHING CAN'T JUST DISAPPEAR LIKE THIS! I DIDN'T GET MY HERO'S ACCLAIM! I DIDN'T GET TO SIGN A SINGLE AUTOGRAPH!

GRANDMA!

HELLO, HAY LIN.

OH, GRANDMA! I'VE MISSED YOU SO MUCH.

ANYONE HAPPEN TO HAVE A TISSUE?

I'M AFRAID NOT, IRMA.

COME HERE, GIRLS.

SNIFF!

YOU DID YOUR DUTY WONDERFULLY. I'M PROUD OF ALL OF YOU.

DOES THAT MEAN OUR MISSION IS OVER?

YES, WILL. AND YOU SUCCEEDED!

THE TASK GIVEN TO YOU FIVE WAS NOT EASY, BUT YOU PROVED YOURSELVES WORTHY OF OUR TRUST.

NOT ONLY DID YOU DEFEND THE VEIL, YOU ALSO HELPED BRING LIFE AND LIGHT BACK TO METAMOOR.

. . . AND DEFEAT ITS NUMBER ONE ENEMY.

ONE DAY I WILL RETURN, AND WHEN THAT DAY COMES, NO ONE WILL BE ABLE TO STOP ME OR SAVE YOU!

MAY THIS VILE GROUP BE EXILED TO THE **TOWER OF MISTS!** THEY MUST REMAIN THERE UNTIL ALL TRACES OF THEIR HATE HAVE VANISHED.

I GUESS WE WON'T BE SEEING THEM FOR A LONG TIME.

THEY ARE NO LONGER YOUR PROBLEM, GUARDIANS. THEY ARE IN CANDRACAR'S CUSTODY NOW.

I HAVE IMAGINED THIS PLACE SO MANY TIMES, BUT I NEVER THOUGHT IT WOULD LOOK LIKE THIS.

I AM SURE YOU HAVE MANY QUESTIONS. WHAT IS THE FIRST THING YOU WOULD LIKE TO KNOW?

THAT GUY NEXT TO YOU . . . IS HE **SANTA CLAUS?**

EXCUSE ME?

OH, JUST IGNORE HER. YOU'RE RIGHT. . . . THERE ARE SO MANY THINGS WE'D LIKE TO KNOW THAT WE'RE NOT SURE WHERE TO START!

THERE WILL COME A TIME FOR ANSWERS, BUT THAT TIME IS NOT NOW.

EVEN THOUGH THIS PART OF YOUR MISSION IS OVER, YOU WILL **CONTINUE** TO BE OUR GUARDIANS. . . .

. . . AND YOU WILL ONE DAY HAVE THE POWER TO FIND THE ANSWERS TO EVERYTHING ON YOUR OWN!

BUT . . .

BUT BE PREPARED— WE MAY NEED YOUR HELP AGAIN IN THE FUTURE.

NOW YOUR POWERS WILL SERVE TO DEFEND NOT ONLY YOUR WORLD BUT ALL OF THE WORLDS UNDER THE WATCHFUL EYE OF CANDRACAR!

AND IT WILL REMAIN THAT WAY UNTIL FIVE NEW GUARDIANS COME TO TAKE YOUR PLACE.

NO WAY! THAT'LL NEVER HAPPEN. WE'LL BE GUARDIANS FOREVER.

SOON YOU WILL RETURN TO YOUR NORMAL LIVES. REMEMBER TO USE YOUR POWERS WISELY.

AND NEVER FORGET WHERE TRUE POWER LIES.

WHAT? TRUE POWER? WAIT, I DON'T UNDERSTAND.

NOT NOW, WILL. THE ORACLE HAS A SERIOUS TASK TO ATTEND TO.

WHAT'S HE DOING?

HE'S ABOUT TO BRING DOWN THE VEIL THAT WAS CREATED LONG AGO TO SEPARATE MERIDIAN FROM THE REST OF THE KNOWN WORLDS. THIS IS AN IMPORTANT MOMENT FOR ALL OF US.

NOW THAT THE THREAT OF PHOBOS IS GONE, THERE'S NO REASON FOR THE VEIL TO REMAIN.

DON'T BE SAD, GIRLS, WE'LL MEET AGAIN. THE HEART OF CANDRACAR WILL HELP YOU RETURN WHENEVER YOU WISH.

YOU ARE WELCOME HERE ANYTIME. AND CANDRACAR SERVES AS THE PASSAGEWAY TO ALL OTHER WORLDS.

GOOD-BYE! DON'T BE AFRAID OF WHAT LIES AHEAD.

WAIT, GRANDMA. CAN'T YOU . . .

. . . TELL US MORE?

IN A HEARTBEAT, IT'S ALL OVER.

I WASN'T EXPECTING TO SEE MY GRANDMA. AND NOW WE KNOW EVEN LESS THAN WE DID AT THE BEGINNING OF THIS WHOLE THING.

HEY, WILL, CAN YOU MAKE THE HEART OF CANDRACAR TAKE US BACK RIGHT NOW?

I THINK WE SHOULD WAIT!

WAIT? WAIT FOR WHAT?

DIDN'T YOU HEAR WHAT THE ORACLE SAID? IT'S NOT TIME FOR ALL THE ANSWERS.

YEAH . . .

. . . AND WHEN THAT TIME COMES, WE'LL BE READY!

SO, NOW WHAT DO WE DO?

I DON'T KNOW ABOUT RIGHT NOW, BUT TOMORROW THERE'S A MATH QUIZ.

THAT'S RIGHT! I TOTALLY FORGOT!

ME, TOO. LET'S SEE IF MRS. RUDOLPH WILL POSTPONE IT UNTIL MONDAY. AFTER ALL, WE DID SAVE HER WORLD. SHE OWES US, BIG-TIME.

HA-HA-HA! I DOUBT THAT'LL HELP US TOO MUCH, IRMA.

COME ON. WHAT DOES A GIRL HAVE TO DO TO AVOID FAILING A QUIZ AT SCHOOL, ANYWAY? SAVE THE ENTIRE UNIVERSE?

NOT A BAD IDEA, BUT WITH OUR LUCK, WE'D END UP HAVING TO DO IT ON A WEEKEND!

HA! HA! HA! HA!